The Berenstain Bears
FLY-IT!

Up, Up, and Away

Random House 🏠 New York

Copyright © 1996 by Berenstain Enterprises, Inc. All rights reserved under International and Pan-American Copyright Conventions. Published in the United States by Random House, Inc., New York, and simultaneously in Canada by Random House of Canada Limited, Toronto. http://www.randomhouse.com/ *Library of Congress Cataloging-in-Publication Data:* Berenstain, Stan, 1923- The Berenstain bears fly-it / by Stan & Jan Berenstain. p. cm. — (First time do-it books) SUMMARY: After visiting the Hall of Flight at the Bearsonian Institution, the Bear cubs decide to invent their own airplanes. Includes information about the history of flight and instructions for making various balloon-powered aircraft. ISBN 0-679-87317-1 (trade). — ISBN 0-679-97317-6 (lib. bdg.) [1. Paper airplanes—Fiction. 2. Inventions—Fiction. 3. Flight—Fiction. 4. Bears—Fiction.] I. Berenstain, Jan, 1923- . II. Title. III. Series: Berenstain, Stan, 1923- First time do-it books. PZ7.B4483Benc 1996 [E]—dc20 96-32906   Printed in the United States of America 10 9 8 7 6 5 4 3 2 1

Sister, Brother, and Cousin Fred were visiting one of their favorite places: the Hall of Flight in the Bearsonian Institution. Many of the most important aircraft in the history of flight were on display, as well as portraits of flight's early heroes.

WILBEAR&ORVILLE WRIGHT

AMELIA BEARHART

INVENTIONS LIKE THE CORKSCREW,

THE MOUSETRAP,

AND THE UMBRELLA GREW OUT OF THE NEED TO SOLVE A PROBLEM.

THE DISCOVERY OF THE MEANS TO FLY DID NOT GROW OUT OF SUCH A NEED, BUT OUT OF THE SPIRIT OF THOSE WHO LONGED TO FLY—OUT OF A SENSE OF THE FREEDOM AND BEAUTY OF FLIGHT.

"Fred," said Brother, "wouldn't it be great if we were Wilbear and Orville Wright and invented the airplane?"

"It sure would," said Fred.

"If you two are going to be Wilbear and Orville Wright, who am I going to be?" asked Sister.

"You can be Amelia Bearhart," said Brother.

"Okay," agreed Sister.

"But it wouldn't do us any good if we were," added Brother, "because all the ideas for inventions have been used up!"

"But that's not true," said Professor Actual Factual. The Bearsonian was his museum, and he had just come into the Hall of Flight.

"Ideas for inventions will never get used up. That's not how inventing works."

THE FIRST IMPORTANT DISCOVERY IN THE HISTORY OF FLIGHT PROBABLY CAME WHEN SOMEONE NOTICED SPARKS RISING.

THAT LED TO THE INVENTION OF THE HOT-AIR BALLOON. BUT THERE ARE ALWAYS DOUBTERS—THOSE WHO POOH-POOH NEW IDEAS.

I SAY THE IDEA OF FLYING IS A LOT OF HOT AIR!

GLIDER
PLUS
GASOLINE ENGINE
EQUALS
AIRPLANE

"Hi, Professor," said Brother. "How *does* inventing work?"

"In different ways," explained the professor. "Sometimes by combining things that have already been invented. Wilbear and Orville put the glider and the gasoline engine together and gave us the airplane."

IT TOOK HUNDREDS OF YEARS TO GET FROM SPARKS RISING FROM A FIRE...

...TO MOTOR-DRIVEN BLIMPS AND DIRIGIBLES.

EXACTLY SO!

"Sometimes an invention comes in a flash," continued Actual Factual. "Almost like a light bulb going on. That's how the paper clip was invented. It was just a bit of wire bent in a new and different way.

JUST AS LIGHTER-THAN-AIR CRAFT WERE INSPIRED BY OBSERVING THE WORKINGS OF NATURE, HEAVIER-THAN-AIR CRAFT WERE INSPIRED BY OBSERVING THE BEAUTIFUL GLIDING FLIGHT OF SEABIRDS.

"And speaking of the light bulb—it was not invented in a flash. Thomas Grizzly Edison knew that an electrical current would make a wire glow. But he had to try hundreds of kinds of wire before he found one that worked."

"Do you think we could invent something, Professor?" asked Sister.

"I do indeed," said Actual Factual. "Just think about the airplane, the paper clip, and the light bulb, and remember this rhyme:

"All inventions,
you will find,
happen first
in someone's mind."

As Sister, Brother, and Fred left the museum, they were thinking about the airplane, the paper clip, and the light bulb. In front of the museum was a park, where all sorts of things were going on. But two of the things jumped out at them and…

AIRCRAFT ENGINES

GASOLINE ENGINE

COMBUSTION OF GASOLINE DRIVES ENGINE, WHICH TURNS PROPELLER, WHICH PULLS AIRPLANE.

JET ENGINE

BURNING OF JET FUEL DRIVES AIRPLANE.

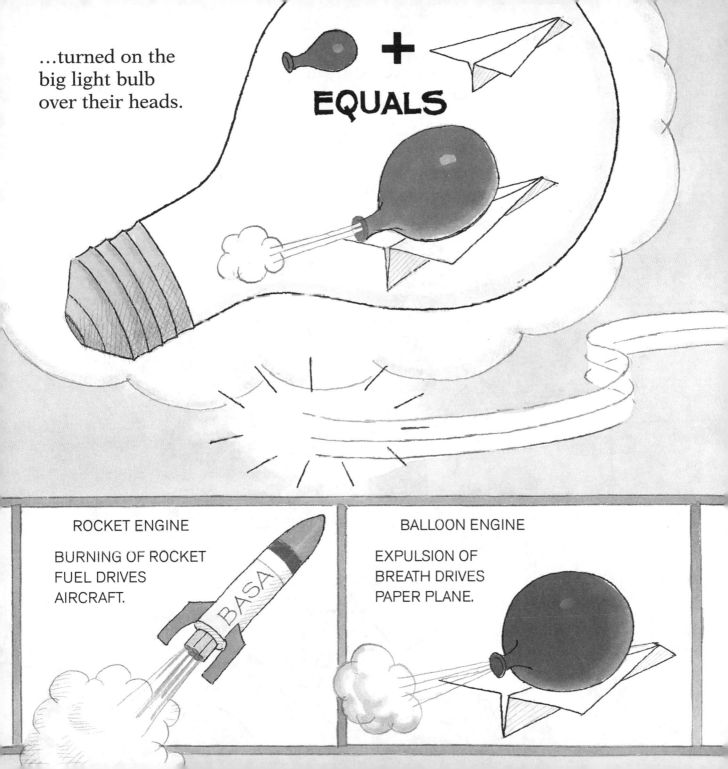

...turned on the big light bulb over their heads.

+

EQUALS

ROCKET ENGINE

BURNING OF ROCKET FUEL DRIVES AIRCRAFT.

BASA

BALLOON ENGINE

EXPULSION OF BREATH DRIVES PAPER PLANE.

The would-be inventors hurried home and went to work.

First, they found a packet of balloons that was left over from Sister's birthday party.

Then they took a sheet of paper and folded it to make a paper plane.

TO BUILD A FLEET OF BREATH POWERED AIRCRAFT YOU WILL NEED

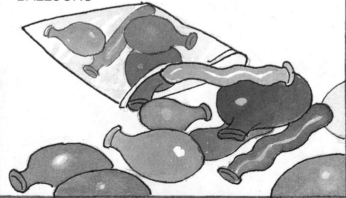

1. DIFFERENT SIZES AND SHAPES OF BALLOONS

2. STICKY TAPE

They blew up a balloon and fastened it to the paper plane with a loop of sticky tape.

Then they launched the first breath-powered aircraft from the front stoop.

3. A VARIETY OF PAPER FROM WHICH TO MAKE PAPER PLANES

4. PLENTY OF BREATH—OR A BALLOON PUMP

A thing of beauty may be a joy forever, but to an inventor...

MOUNTING THE ENGINE

1. BLOW UP BALLOON. HOLD NOZZLE TO PREVENT LOSS OF POWER.

2. MAKE LOOP OUT OF STICKY TAPE (STICKY SIDE OUT).

...an invention that works the first time is a thrill that comes once in a lifetime.

3. FIX LOOP TO PAPER PLANE

4. STILL HOLDING NOZZLE CLOSED, ATTACH BALLOON TO TAPE.

5. LET 'ER FLY!

Just as Wilbear and Orville Wright improved on their invention by trying different designs, Sister, Brother, and Fred improved their invention by trying different combinations of balloons and paper planes.

They made a speedster by combining a small, tough balloon with a racing-style paper plane.

PAPER PLANE DESIGN

BASIC PAPER PLANE CONSTRUCTION

1.

2.

3.

4.

DOTTED LINES INDICATE FOLDS.

They made a giant two-motor airliner by mounting two large balloons on a paper plane made of newspaper.

RACING PAPER PLANE CONSTRUCTION

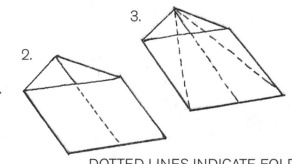

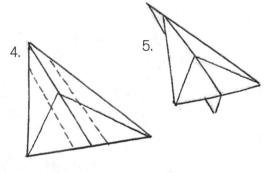

DOTTED LINES INDICATE FOLDS.

Every time they tried something different, they learned something new.

They learned that sausage-powered planes flew straight and true,

that a spiral-powered plane wiggled and shivered,

EXPERIMENTAL PLANES	WHISPER JET	SILVER STREAK
	TWIN MOTORS MOUNTED ON PAPER WINGS ATTACHED TO SAUSAGE-SHAPED BALLOON	SAUSAGE MOTOR MOUNTED ON RACING ALUMINUM FOIL PLANE
		ALUMINUM FOIL

and that a two-motored banana loop-the-looped.

P-38

TWO RACING PAPER PLANES TAPED TOGETHER WITH A REAR-MOUNTED MOTOR

PIECE OF STRAW TAPED HERE

FLYING BANANA

LARGE CURVED YELLOW BALLOON WITH TWO UNDERSLUNG MOTORS

FOR BANANA EFFECT, ADD SPOTS WITH BLACK MARKER.

They learned that some breath-powered aircraft have minds of their own. One turned on Brother and chased him around the tree house.

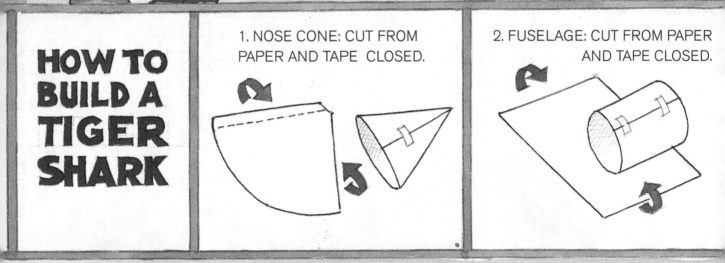

HOW TO BUILD A TIGER SHARK

1. NOSE CONE: CUT FROM PAPER AND TAPE CLOSED.

2. FUSELAGE: CUT FROM PAPER AND TAPE CLOSED.

Another landed in a nest and was attacked by a mama robin.

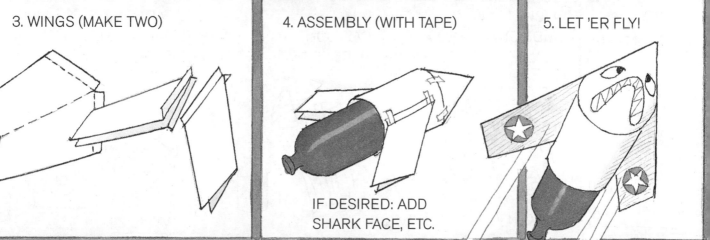

3. WINGS (MAKE TWO)

4. ASSEMBLY (WITH TAPE)

IF DESIRED: ADD SHARK FACE, ETC.

5. LET 'ER FLY!

Just as others built on the successes of Wilbear and Orville Wright, others built on Sister, Brother, and Fred's successes.

Sister's friend Lizzy Bruin made an ascension balloon that came down by parachute.

| ASCENSION BALLOON CONSTRUCTION | 1. CUT SIX INCH-WIDE STRIPS FROM NEWSPAPER. | 2. MAKE BALLOON HARNESS. | 3. MAKE PARACHUTE WITH THREAD, GLUE, AND A TISSUE. | 4. TAPE PARACHU TO HARNE |

Lizzy's brother, Barry, made a terrific model of the Goodbear blimp using one big balloon and two small ones.

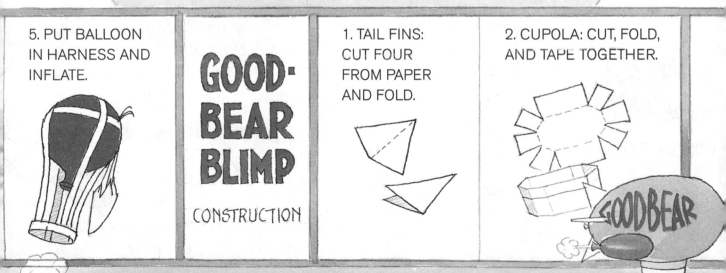

5. PUT BALLOON IN HARNESS AND INFLATE.

GOOD-BEAR BLIMP

CONSTRUCTION

1. TAIL FINS: CUT FOUR FROM PAPER AND FOLD.

2. CUPOLA: CUT, FOLD, AND TAPE TOGETHER.

The Too-Tall gang made a pirate's space station that flew the Jolly Roger.

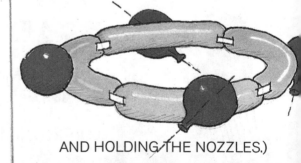

1. TAPE FOUR INFLATED CURVED BALLOONS TOGETHER.

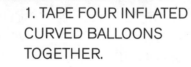

2. ATTACH FOUR MOTORS WITH NOZZLES ANGLED DOWN. (YOU'LL NEED HELP INFLATING THEM...

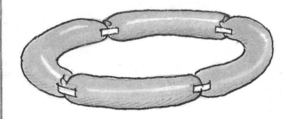

AND HOLDING THE NOZZLES.)

Professor Actual Factual's nephew, super-smart Ferdy Factual, made a three-stage rocket that actually worked.

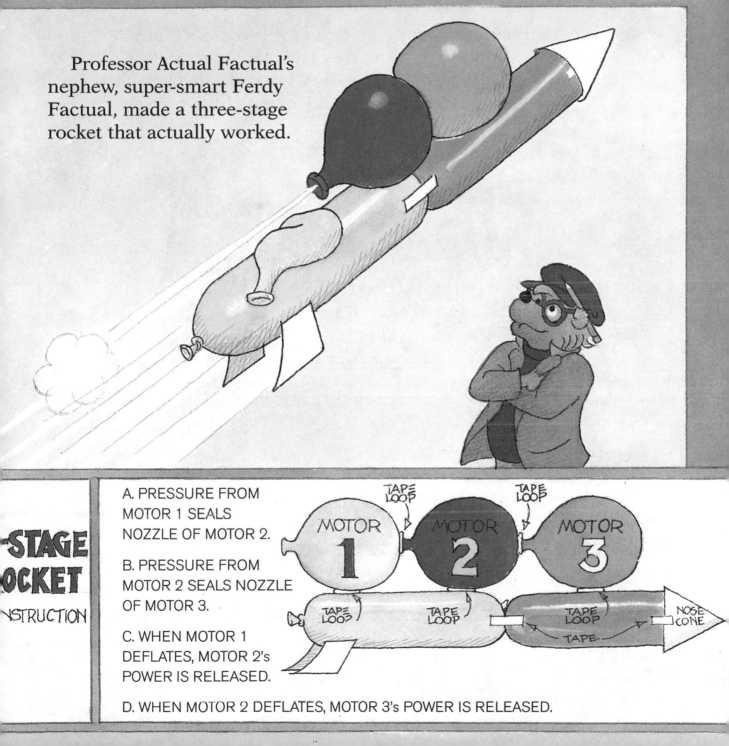

A. PRESSURE FROM MOTOR 1 SEALS NOZZLE OF MOTOR 2.

B. PRESSURE FROM MOTOR 2 SEALS NOZZLE OF MOTOR 3.

C. WHEN MOTOR 1 DEFLATES, MOTOR 2's POWER IS RELEASED.

D. WHEN MOTOR 2 DEFLATES, MOTOR 3's POWER IS RELEASED.

It had been an exciting day for inventors Sister, Brother, and Fred, and they had learned a lot. But the most important thing they learned was the message in Professor Actual Factual's little poem.

ALL INVENTIONS,
YOU WILL FIND,
HAPPEN FIRST
IN SOMEONE'S MIND.

WHERE TO FLY BREATH-POWERED AIRCRAFT
OUTDOORS AND INDOORS

BREATH-POWERED AIRCRAFT NEED WIND-FREE CONDITIONS TO FLY OUTDOORS. WIND IS WEAKEST EARLY IN THE MORNING AND AT SUNDOWN.

BREATH-POWERED AIRCRAFT ARE EXCELLENT INDOOR FLIERS. LARGE, HIGH-CEILINGED ROOMS ARE BEST. LARGE LIVING ROOMS, SCHOOL GYMS AND AUDITORIUMS, AND LOBBIES ARE IDEAL. BUT ONLY WITH PERMISSION.

NOTE OF CAUTION!
VERY YOUNG CHILDREN MUST NEVER BE ALLOWED TO PUT BALLOONS OR BITS OF BROKEN BALLOONS IN THEIR MOUTHS!

KEEP 'EM FLYIN'!